# CASTAWAY CROWN

## (MATTHEW AND ANNA'S UNDERSEA ADVENTURE)

## ROSANNA GARTLEY

A Mouse Gate Adventure™

Mouse Gate Press
1103 Middlecreek
Friendswood, Texas 77546
281-992-3131 TEL
www.MouseGate.com

ISBN:   978-1-59095-353-2
UPC:   6-43977-43533-0

Printed in the United States of America with simultaneous printings in Australia, Canada, and the United Kingdom.

FIRST EDITION
1   2   3   4   5   6   7   8   9   10

Cover art from fotolia by Natali Snailcat and Olga Naidenova

*Dedicated to our first born grandson, Matthew and his sister, Anna, our first born granddaughter. Your loving personalities and amazing talents make me proud!*

*—Grandma Rosie*

## Acknowledgments

Thanks to my husband, John for all his support; my editor, Sigrid Macdonald and my publisher, TotalRecall Publications, Inc.

## The Book

Matthew and Anna are full of excitement when they learn their family is going on a Disney cruise. With the magic of Disney both children are propelled into an adventure far below the ocean when they are asked to help the sea creatures get rid of a bothersome ghost. With Matthew's above average intellect coupled with Anna's amazing drawing abilities they solve the two hundred-year-old mystery bringing peace to the sea and the ghost.

# Chapter 1

## (Europe, 1789)

"Yes, ma' lady," said Mary as she curtsied in front of the queen.

"Mary, I have a very special task for you. There is a ship sailing to New Spain. It has been said that this land has the purest of silver and the most dazzling gems anywhere in the world. As you know, I have yet to command that a crown be made for myself since I married King Oscar. It must be worthy enough to be put upon my head and to be handed down to my heirs."

"Yes, ma'am, and my duty?"

"You are to be on that ship, and when it docks in New Spain, you will oversee the mining of the silver and gemstones. Then you will supervise the making, by hand, of my exquisite crown. I would like to take care of such work myself, but the journey is far too arduous for a creature as delicate as myself."

"Yes, ma'am, when does this journey begin?"

"The ship sails in two days. Be on it!"

"How long will I be on board the ship, and how long until I am brought back home?"

"Questions! Too many questions! How shall I know the details? Go talk to the king—surely he can explain it all to you."

"Yes, ma'am." Mary was used to being treated harshly. She had been the queen's lady-in-waiting long before the queen had attained her title. Mary had wet-nursed Her Royal Highness, Louisa, from the day she was born. As Louisa grew, Mary became her governess, and when she married the Royal Prince, Oscar, Mary had become her lady-in-waiting. When the prince's father passed, Oscar became king, and Louisa became queen.

Mary had loved Louisa forever. She had spent more time with the child than Louisa's own mother—which was quite usual in wealthy households. Grown women had much to attend to besides rearing their children. Louisa had been a rosy-cheeked, blonde-haired, blue-eyed cherub with a sparkling personality. The child had been loving, kind, and respectful, and she and Mary had been almost inseparable. It wasn't until Louisa entered her teens that her attitude changed to being self-centered, selfish, and almost unapproachable. Sadly, her less than civil personality followed her right to the throne. It was hard for Mary to believe that this difficult woman was the same sweet girl she had nurtured for the past nineteen years.

Mary was no longer a young woman, and the

journey across the ocean would be long and filled with hardship and sacrifice. She was afraid that her weary body would not be able to overcome the terrible accommodations, sparse food and water, seasickness, the constant threat of bad weather and deadly assaults by pirates. She wasted no time in finding the king as she had been instructed. He, unlike his wife, was always approachable, treating the servants with respect. Secretly, she wondered what could have attracted Oscar to Louisa.

King Oscar was in the royal library. It was the coziest room in the castle. The king had come from a learned family, one that valued education. He had loved books and reading since he was a child, and in the evenings, he could often be found sitting near the fireplace with an open book before him. Such was the case on this night. Mary paused at the library's heavy oak door, but the king, so absorbed in his book, did not notice her presence.

Mary cleared her throat and said, "My Lord." He looked up from the page.

"Come, come," said King Oscar, beckoning her to move forward while he put his thumb between the pages to keep his place before closing the book.

"I'm terribly sorry to bother you, my Lord, but ma'am suggested I find you and ask about the details regarding the voyage to New Spain," said Mary, her eyes never leaving the floor out of respect.

"I'm the one who is sorry. I'm sorry my wife is dragging you into her cockamamie scheme to get a new crown. There is nothing wrong with the crown my mother wore as queen. In fact, it is cloaked in history, and Louisa should be proud to wear it."

"Yes, sir," replied Mary, as she became privy to some unflattering comments from the king about the queen, which made her uncomfortable.

"But you know her quite possibly better than I do. You know there will be no peace until she gets the crown she wants," carried on the king.

"Yes, ma' Lord." And then King Oscar invited Mary to sit with him while he gave her all the information he knew about the voyage's details. Armed with the necessary knowledge, Mary knew she had much to do the next day to ready herself for the journey. She dreaded crossing the ocean. Had she been twenty years younger, she would have found it to be a great adventure. But she would do it for Louisa—only because she was the queen, and Louisa had given Mary a straightforward command.

It was nearly impossible for Mary to know what to wear or to pack. Most of her clothing was hand-made as she was considered part of society's upper crust. The queen and Mary shared the same dressmaker. Because she was to be handsomely dressed at all times in public, she did not own any clothing that was not elegant, and there was certainly no time to have any sewn.

The start of the voyage necessitated that she wear a rather warm and heavy ensemble. She had chosen an olive-toned dress made of finely spun wool. Under the dress, along with her bustier and petticoat, she wore her smallest hoop and bustle. Without knowing about the accommodations over the next few months, she felt it was reasonable to make her skirt flare as little as possible. The dress had been sewn to include a matching full-length cape. No doubt the sea air would be cold, and a warm cape would be welcome. Mary's standing in society made it imperative that she wear a hat designed by the best milliner, of course. It would not keep her warm but would indicate her standing in the community. She had heard that New Spain was summery warm year-round, so she packed numerous dresses made from cotton and silk, hoping the fabrics would help her tolerate the heat.

With her steamer trunks packed full of her belongings and as much food and drink as she could manage, she was driven by horse and carriage to the port where the ship awaited. The day was bright and sunny yet cool. After all, it was only early spring. Long before the horse and buggy reached the shore, she could see the tall ship's masts swaying in the harbor. The masts were massive, and she could only imagine how large the sails would be once they were unfurled. The ship itself, the Rosa Marie, was not large, nor was it grand or even comfortable. It had been designed and built, along with many others, as a trade packet ship. It and its crew were to carry mail, supplies, and to fit in as many passengers as possible among its cargo as a way of making more money during each journey. The crew's quarters were very rough—stark yet adequate—and the paying passengers' staterooms were nearly the same. Each compact room featured a bed and a small dresser.

Mary saw to it that her trunks had been brought on board. Her name had been crossed off the passenger list as the sailor looked at her from top to bottom—wondering why this well-to-do woman was boarding a ship like this one. Her heart sank as she stepped from the dock to the upper deck. Once aboard, she had no trouble finding her assigned room. Her room did not have a porthole, and she was thankful for she had heard how badly they leaked in rough seas.

She stood at the ship's rail, watching the other passengers embark while the crew finished loading their cargo. She thought ahead to what the journey might be like. She knew, because of the time of year, that the Atlantic Ocean would be very cold with ice floes still visible above the surface. They would be sailing south-west, and the weather would become more welcoming as the journey continued. She had heard that New Spain's climate made it possible for beautiful palm trees and lush flowers to grow without so much as a gardener's care. She had heard about sandy beaches where one could sit and watch the waves or even swim in them. Mary had once read a book that described the tropical fruits that grew there, right on the trees, ready to be picked. It was the thought of these things that Mary wanted to experience. Of course, she would deal with the crown, but she would make sure she treated herself to the things she had only heard about.

Mary was pleased to see other women coming aboard although each one had been on the arm of a gentleman. A woman travelling anywhere alone was nearly unheard of in the kingdom, but Mary was the queen's lady-in-waiting, a very prestigious title—one that she hoped would bring her respect on the ship. The king had sent a letter with Mary, explaining her role once in New Spain and demanding that she receive all the help she would need to fulfill her duty to the queen.

By the time she watched the crew untie the massive ropes that had tethered the ship to the dock, she had resigned herself to the voyage. She would return with Queen Louisa's crown.

# Chapter 2

Several weeks had passed since Mary had begun the voyage to New Spain. Much of the time she had spent lying in her bunk trying to calm her stomach from the ravaging, relentless sea sickness brought on by the listing seas. Most of the other passengers were likewise affected, yet the captain and his crew carried on working, eating, and drinking as if on dry land. Unable to eat, Mary was losing weight. Her clothes were looser, and common sense told her she had to be able to keep nourishment in her stomach to stay strong and repel disease, or she would not survive.

Storm after storm tossed the small ship like a toy, but miraculously the vessel stayed afloat. Finally, the seas calmed. Mary emerged from her room and headed for the deck for some much needed fresh air. By mid-morning, most of the passengers were enjoying the sunshine and open space. It was as if they had all been released from prison. The common joy they felt urged them to mingle and converse with each other. From talking to fellow passengers, Mary found that there was a wide variety of differing reasons for the journey among those on board. Some of the men were heading to New Spain to find work in the booming silver mines. Wealthier couples were hoping to experience a new land and culture that they had only read about. Others were merely seeking adventure with no itinerary at all. Mary's shipmates expressed awe when she revealed the purpose of her trip. She was the closest thing to royalty any of them had ever met.

The next several weeks of calm weather brought good humor and better health to some on board. When the captain said that by his calculations, they were over halfway to Tampico, New Spain, there was a loud cheer from the passengers and the crew alike.

The following weeks were not without peril. The ship and its passengers endured many squalls and dangers from sea life. Pods of humpback whales caused the captain concern as they remained swimming off the starboard side of the ship for days. It was a relief when he saw their breaching farther and farther away from the ship. Mary liked watching the enormous sea creatures. She had come to know which adults belonged to which calves, and their presence made her feel less alone on the vast ocean.

During her voyage, Mary had grown used to seasickness in herself and those around her. She learned that it was the least of the afflictions on board. Having lived a protected life within the castle walls, she had never been exposed to the horrors she witnessed during the ten-week trip.

The young children were the most vulnerable to the measles and smallpox, not to mention the hunger and lack of safe drinking water. Many young people died during the trip. Mary witnessed the parents' grief as their children's lifeless bodies were thrown overboard into the sea; it was more than heart-breaking. Those that ended up ill often endured weeks of debilitating pain as they lay in their own vomit and feces with lice so thick on their bodies the insects could be scraped off.

Once Mary had consumed the food she had brought on board, she was forced to eat from the ship's provisions. The heavily salted food caused painful mouth sores and boils on her lips and face. The lack of decent nourishment caused more deaths, and the horror she once felt at watching bodies being tossed overboard turned into a daily expectation. The stench on board worsened each day despite the efforts of the crew. But swabbing the decks and living quarters with sea water did nothing to squelch the diseases that continued to spread on board.

Finally, the land of New Spain was in sight. For Mary, it was a relief, but for many it was not. Mary had come prepared with enough gold to secure her release from the ship. Others had not and were forced to remain on board until they were purchased by someone in the new land. In turn for their passage to New Spain, many were forced to agree to work for a specified time for those who paid their way off the ship—a type of slavery. During this process, families were often split up, and those on board the ship who were too ill to work were left to die in their own filth.

Mary was indeed eager to pay her fare and get off the ship as fast as possible. King Oscar and Queen Louisa had sent word with Mary to the Bourbon family, who took over the governing of New Spain, informing them the reason for Mary's arrival. The aristocratic leader, then, sent horse and carriage for the lady-in-waiting, putting her up in private quarters.

It was weeks before Mary was healthy enough to pursue her given tasks. With multiple baths using lye soap, and healthy food and drink, she began to feel clean, rested, and nourished once again. It was only then that she made herself available to oversee the mining of the jewels and the silver necessary for the making of Queen Louisa's crown.

During her year in New Spain, Mary was kept busy. She was transported to various silver mines to watch the metal being removed from the earth. Although she knew absolutely nothing about the mining or the refining process, she performed her duty by being on site. The miners were unimpressed with a woman being allowed into their world, and Mary would have liked to have been almost anywhere else but in the filthy mines and refineries.

Witnessing the mining of the gems was somewhat more interesting. Once they were cut and polished, their beauty was revealed. It was her job to select the number and type of jewels to be inlaid into her majesty's crown, which was indeed magnificent. The multiple peaks of silver were each topped with a unique jewel. The finest emeralds, rubies, fire opals, topaz, and amethyst were mined, cut with many facets, and then placed within the silver. As she watched the completion of the piece, Mary realized she would be on her way home sooner than later. The thought of the dismal, wretched conditions that she would have to endure on the ship for a second time made her stomach turn. She had been treated well by her host—far better than Louisa treated her—and she did not look forward to leaving New Spain. But once the leather craftsman finished the hand-made box that would protect the crown, she could no longer prolong the beginning of her voyage home.

This time, besides the crew, there were fewer passengers on board, making the conditions somewhat better. Less crowding meant more food to go around and less chance of disease being passed from person to person. As the beautiful sun shimmered on the turquoise Caribbean Sea and the fresh air blew through her hair, Mary said good-bye to the land that had become special to her. Sadly, she would never see this land or her homeland again.

# Chapter 3

## (Canada, 2016)

It was wintertime on the Canadian prairies. Despite the children's love of hockey and skating lessons, the cold and snowy season seemed long. The need for multiple layers of clothing, having to wear mitts, scarves, and toques which often ended up in the school's lost and found, as well as having to be bundled in big bulky boots and coats, made it feel as though winter would never end. At least the February school break would provide some relief from trudging through the snow on the way to school every day. Anna and Matthew were excited for the upcoming school vacation as they clomped into the house on Friday afternoon. After kicking off their boots, which made snow fly all over the wall near the back door, they quickly peeled off their snow pants and the remainder of their winter gear. Anna wondered if there was time for her to watch a movie before dinner.

"Mom, Mom?" yelled Anna.

"I'm down here," answered her mom.

"Where?" asked Anna.

"Down in the basement. Come down, and give me a hand."

"Okay," said Anna, approaching the stairs. She reached the bottom and saw four suitcases sitting on the basement floor.

"Grab a couple of these, please, Anna, and take them to the bedrooms."

"Suitcases? What for, Mom? Are we going somewhere?"

"Yes, we are, but you have to wait until Dad comes home to find out the details."

"C'mon, Mom."

"Nope. Your dad should be home soon," said Mom as she tousled Anna's short, blonde, curly hair on the way by her with two more suitcases.

Anna lugged two of the suitcases up to the kitchen.

"Keep going, Anna. Take them up to the bedrooms."

Matthew was lying on his bed reading when he heard something being wheeled along the hallway. Sitting up on his Pittsburgh Penguins comforter, he stretched his neck to see what the noise was.

"Suitcases? What are those for?" Their mom continued on to the master suite while Anna placed a piece of luggage next to her brother's bed.

"I don't know," said Anna. "Mom won't tell us till Dad gets home."

Glancing at his watch, Matthew said, "He should be home soon. Did you and Mom bring up four suitcases?"

"Yep," replied Anna.

"Hmm, that means we are going somewhere far away," reasoned Matthew. "When we go to the city, we only take one or two."

"That's right!" squealed Anna letting her imagination wander. "Where do you think we're going?"

"Well," said Matthew, thoughtfully, "four big suitcases, and we don't have school for ten more days. I think we're going to fly somewhere— maybe somewhere warm."

"I'll bet we're going back to Cuba," said Anna.

"Mom and Dad liked it there—I'll bet you're right!"

"Hurry home, Dad. Hurry home," said Anna, jumping up and down.

Max, their black lab, got up from beside Matthew's bed and made his way to sit at the back door, a sure sign that Dad had pulled into the driveway. The kids ran from Matthew's room to the door nearly toppling over the big dog, and being in the way for the door to open, all the while bombarding their dad with questions he couldn't yet hear.

"Whoa, you two," said Dad, knowing full well why the kids were excited.

"Mom, Dad's home," yelled Anna. Mom came down from the bedrooms, and Anna saw her give Dad a wink.

"C'mon, you guys. Where are we going? You gotta put me and Anna out of our misery," pleaded Matthew. It was clear that their parents were dragging this out for dramatic effect, and Matthew was having none of it!

"All right," said Mom. "Let's all sit down." As everyone became seated, Mom began: "You know you have next week off, so Dad and I took the week off too. I'm tired of the cold. How about you guys?"

"I'm ready for a beach," said Matthew.

"I think you will be able to go to several beaches," said Mom, giving the kids a hint.

"Several beaches? Are we going to more than one place?"

"In a way."

"What does that mean?" asked Anna.

"We will be taken to several beaches."

"Huh?" said Anna, more confused than ever.

"We're going on a Disney cruise!" explained Dad.

"What?!" said Matthew.

"Tomorrow, we will go to the city and fly to Orlando. On Sunday, we will board the ship."

The trip was beyond either child's expectations. They had been fortunate enough to be on a cruise before—they could not have been more excited.

# Chapter 4

The flight to Orlando went as planned, and before they knew it, they were greeted by Disney characters as they boarded the ship. They easily found their stateroom, and this time Matthew claimed the upper bunk. Anna didn't mind; she was so excited to be there, she would have happily slept on the floor. Lunch was being served, so the family decided to eat first, then explore the ship.

Disney characters were all over the ship welcoming the guests. Even though Anna and Matthew knew they were actors dressed up, they loved having their pictures taken with characters they had only seen on TV or in the movies. Anna was particularly impressed with the beautiful ball gowns worn by the princesses.

Lunch was delicious, and after walking around the ship, the kids just couldn't decide what to do first. Their luggage had yet to make it to their room, so swimming would have to wait. Then they heard an announcement regarding the safety drill. It seemed sensible to wait until that was over before doing anything else. By the time the muster drill ended, and the passengers had been dismissed, the family's luggage had been placed in their room.

The Orlando air was a bit cool, but to those used to temperatures far below zero, it felt like a summer's day. The family decided that they would start their voyage in one of the ship's swimming pools. It had been months since Matthew and Anna had been swimming, and they made the most of the opportunity by playing in the pool for hours. Soon the city was far behind them, and all there was to see was the vast ocean as they made their way to the warm Caribbean. As the rest of the day wound down, the hours of swimming and the excitement had made the family tired. No one complained about bedtime as the kids were tucked in while wondering what tomorrow would bring. That was their last thought as they drifted off to sleep, feeling the slight sway of the ship on the waves.

There was no sleeping in for this family. Long before dressing, they had been out on their balcony watching the ocean go by. Now, they could see islands here and there. The day's itinerary indicated they would dock in the Bahamas at Disney's private island, Castaway Cay. The information printed about the cay gave them many choices as to how to spend their day. One thing the whole family agreed on was to rent snorkeling gear and see what was below the waves. Anna and Matthew had never snorkeled before, but it didn't take them long to get used to the mask, snorkel, and flippers. They began on the Discover Trail—meant for beginners. Anna got so excited when she saw the first school of blue tang that she forgot her mouth was underwater. She began to point and yell at Matthew to look, but all she got was a mouthful of ocean. Sputtering and coughing out the salty water, she quickly put her snorkel back in her mouth ready to continue exploring the amazing world below.

After an hour, it was time for a break. The warm sun and sand felt like a good place to relax. While Mom and Dad lounged on chaises, the kids began shell collecting on the beach, placing their treasures in their red and white beach bags. They ate lunch on the beach, then went back into the water to snorkel the Explorer Trail. Once again, they couldn't believe the beauty of the creatures and plants that lived below the sea. They headed to the beach for more rest, and then it was time to get back on the ship.

The sun and surf had played out the whole family. Evidence they had played in the sun was visible on each family member but more so on Anna. Her very pale skin, despite its layer of sunscreen, had turned red. It was a little sore, so her mom applied some soothing lotion. Tomorrow, she would stay out of the sun.

# Chapter 5

The next day was spent at sea, cruising to another wonderful Caribbean island. Anna and her mom spent time together out of the sun, which was not difficult. They participated in several onboard activities. They played bingo and went to the spa for the full treatment of facials, manicures, and pedicures. They tried their luck in the arcade, and then they had a lovely lunch. Following a short nap, they watched a live show, then dressed for dinner. It would only be the two of them as Dad and Matthew had decided to continue water sliding and eat burgers by the pool.

Mom and Anna waited for a table in the restaurant and were happy to see their personal waiter, Pan, standing beside their table. After being seated, Pan explained that if Anna wanted to draw a picture on a placemat, her art would be displayed using Disney magic on the many screens beside each table. Yes, she wanted to draw a picture! Drawing was Anna's main hobby. She loved to draw, and many thought she was very good at it too. She almost forgot about eating as she began creating an underwater scene featuring the sea creatures she had become fascinated with while snorkeling the day before. Her drawing was spectacular! Anna's natural artistic ability prompted her to recall many of the fish and to draw them realistically. The completed picture was colorful and closely resembled what she had seen below the sea.

Pan took their order for dinner, and Anna completed her picture just as their food was served. Pan made sure the drawing was given to the right person so it could be put on display. Anna kept a close eye on the screen beside their table. She was beginning to wonder if she would see it at all before they finished dessert when her picture flashed onto the screens, and that was when something magical happened!

Meanwhile, Matthew and his dad had spent all day sitting in the sun, swimming, playing water polo and water basketball in the various pools, and water sliding—Matthew's favorite! They were both a little waterlogged when Dad thought they should head back to their stateroom and catch up with Mom and Anna.

"Just one more trip down the slide, Dad, please," begged Matthew.

"Okay, but this is your last time for today, bud."

Matthew climbed the stairs for the thirty-sixth time that day. This time, he would try to go down faster than ever before. He lay down flat, crossing his arms over his chest and crossing his ankles, hoping to decrease any wind resistance that might slow him down. As he picked up momentum, he knew he was going faster than before. He closed his eyes while he hooted and hollered with excitement. As he hit the water, something magical happened!

When he opened his eyes, he was entirely under water but not in the ship's swimming pool. Instead, he was in the vast depths of the Caribbean Sea, heading toward the ocean floor. Matthew began to panic, scrambling to stop sinking and start swimming to reach the surface. That is until he heard a familiar voice.

"It's okay, Matthew. We're fine." It was Anna, she was beside him.

"What's going on, Anna?"

"I'm not sure, but I think it's Disney magic. Look, you have a wet suit on, and you can talk and breathe underwater—just like I can."

"Look down, Anna! Look what's happening!" As Anna listened to her brother, she looked down and discovered that she was being covered in scales from the waist down. Each scale formed perfectly on top of one another until her feet disappeared and a beautiful, elegant fish tail had taken their place. By the time the transformation was complete, she was covered in iridescent purple scales and had become a beautiful mermaid.

Where there had been fear, the brother and

sister now only experienced wonder and curiosity. They no longer questioned where they were and why but were relaxing together in an environment they couldn't wait to explore. As they swam along, each chunk of coral or rock they passed offered a new scene, like something out of a movie. The coral and fish were even more beautiful than they had seen snorkeling.

"Do you think the ship is above us?" asked Anna.

"Maybe," replied Matthew, "but I don't know for sure."

"If you don't mind me interrupting, I can tell you your ship is nowhere near here." Startled, Anna grabbed Matthew's hand and looked around to see where the voice was coming from. There was plenty of coral swaying in the undersea current but not much else.

"Who said that?" asked Matthew.

"Me," said the voice.

"Look, Anna, I think it's that little fish with the long white fins."

"Where?"

"Over there, hiding behind that rock."

"Yes, it's me," said the fish, cautiously looking around and then quickly darting over to the humans.

"You're a fish, and you can talk?" asked Anna.

"Yes, it's the same magic that lets you breathe underwater. I should introduce myself. I'm Angela, and I'm an angel fish."

"I thought you might be because of your long

floaty fins and because you're white."

"Angel fish come in lots of spectacular colors. Some of us even have dots or stripes. I'm just plain white. I'll introduce you to some of my colorful cousins. I'm sure we will run into them at some point. Anyway, down here in the Caribbean Sea, we've been expecting you."

"Expecting us?" exclaimed Matthew. "How can that be?"

"I can't really explain it, but we've known for some time that you would be coming to help us."

"I don't understand. How can we help you?"

"We have quite a problem, and you two have what it takes to solve it. But first, I am going to take a day or two and show you both around, you know, help you get your bearings. I also want to introduce you to the others that live around here. We have had the problem for over two hundred years, so if we take another day or two to get acquainted, it won't exactly matter." Once Angela began swimming with the two newcomers, other sea life became visible. Fish began to slowly show themselves from between rocks, from being buried in the sand of the ocean floor, and from hiding in the coral.

"Wow, look at all the beautiful fish!" said Anna.

"Now that they know you're not dangerous, they aren't afraid. But please keep your eyes open for our enemies."

"What should we watch for?"

"Always watch for eels in the rocks and, of course, sharks. We also have a problem with lionfish, barracuda, cobia, and swordfish. Small fish like me are most in danger. The bigger you are down here, the safer you are. If you are small, you have to be fast and know where the hiding places are." Anna and Matthew looked at each other with fear etched on their faces. "We all look out for each other down here, so don't worry. Ready for a tour?"

# Chapter 6

The magnificence of the undersea environment quickly replaced the fear the siblings had been feeling. They could hardly believe what they were seeing. The plants and the coral were just about as beautiful as anything they had seen on dry land, and they told Angela so.

"This reef is part of the second largest reef in the world. Only the Great Barrier Reef off the coast of Australia is larger," informed Angela.

"I always thought coral was kind of white and hard like a rock," admitted Anna, as she watched the red lace-like coral swaying in the current. The coral growing beside it resembled a large bouquet of tightly-packed, brilliant orange flowers, and the beige coral looked just like human brains. Matthew had read about the ocean when he studied it in school, but he never dreamt it actually looked like it did. The colors were astonishing. Purple, orange, shades of pink, red, brown, yellow, and gold made the reef look like a giant flower garden. Then there were the spotted brown, gray, and black rocks. Their crevices and holes made great homes for darker colored creatures that needed a place to hide.

As they swam toward the orange coral, a clownfish passed them by. Taking a second look, Anna asked, "Was that Nemo?"

"Yes, it was. But don't expect him to stop and talk. Now that he is a celebrity, he is always busy. I haven't had a long conversation with him in years," explained Angela.

"Wow!" said Anna.

Swimming by some white coral, Angel said, "Hi, Puff."

"Hi, Ange." Matthew and Anna looked around to see where the voice had come from.

"Who said that?" whispered Anna to Angela.

"My friend, Puff. Look closely in the white coral." Sure enough, once she focused on the coral, she could see two eyes looking at her.

"Puff is a Puffer fish. He doesn't move too fast anymore because he has asthma and has to use his puffer frequently. He mostly stays hidden, out of the sight of predators."

"Fascinating," said Matthew. A colorful school of fish was approaching from the side. Wondering if Angela would introduce them, Matthew slowed down, but all Angela did was wave a fin at them as they slipped silently by.

"Those are pretty," commented Anna.

"Yes, they are. They are goldfish, and their name has gone to their heads."

"What do you mean?"

"They think they are worth a lot of money—you know, precious because of their name. They think they are made of twenty-four karat gold.

We've tried to explain it to them, but they think they know better. They always act like they are better than the rest of us." As they continued on their tour, Angela said hello to various creatures that were so well camouflaged that the trio had swum by them before Matthew or Anna could point them out.

"Look down," said Angela. "Hey, you two, I want you to meet these two."

"Hi, Ange," said the talking sand.

"Matthew and Anna, I'd like for you to meet the twin starfish. This one is Twinkle, and her sister is Shine."

"Hi," said the brother and sister.

"Twins, this is Matthew and Anna—the help we've been expecting."

"We are so excited you're here," said Shine.

"We gotta go," announced Angela. "See you two later."

Swimming around a large rock, they came upon a small cave-like structure where several types of fish were huddled near the entrance.

"What's going on here?" asked Matthew.

"This is our local hospital. Predators, the coral, and, of course, fishermen can cause wounds that need medical attention. You see that dark gray fish? That is a doctor fish. Many of them have disappeared because you humans are using them in your spas to eat dead skin off human feet so that the feet become smooth and beautiful again. But we need them down here, as you can imagine. The larger, bright blue fish with the yellow tail is our surgeon fish, and the very slender brown fish are the needle fish. They do a great job of stitching up anything that is torn. They usually hang out near the surface, but when we need them, they come down in a hurry. The very large fish you see is our nurse shark. You can tell by the name that it is also part of our medical team. Its job is to patrol the area around the medical center to make sure predators don't take advantage of our injured or sick marine life."

"So how do the needle fish know when to come down and help?" asked Matthew.

"I'm glad you asked. That's when the trumpet fish come in handy. I don't see any right now, but they are long and skinny, either orange or yellow, and their mouths look much like trumpets. They sound different notes to warn us of things or to make announcements. Once the needle fish hear certain notes, they come down to help."

"Kind of like a human getting paged or hearing a siren."

"There is so much more to show you, so many more of my friends and neighbors to introduce you to, but perhaps it's time to take a break and let you catch your breath," said Angela, laughing hysterically. "Catch your breath, get it?" she said while swimming in circles.

"Ha-ha, we get it," said Anna, smiling while shaking her head and rolling her eyes.

"You guys hungry?" asked Angela.

"Now that you mention it, I am a little, but

what can we eat down here?" asked Anna looking at the fish swimming by. "Sushi?"

"No, not sushi! But I could take you to the Krusty Krab."

"You mean for real?" asked Matthew.

"Of course, for real. We get tired eating plankton just like anybody else."

"You mean, there really is a Bikini Bottom?" asked Anna.

"Of course, they didn't just pick the name out of thin air."

"Do SpongeBob and Patrick live there like in the cartoon?"

"Sure, and Squidward. They are all our neighbors."

"Wow, where do you live?" asked Anna.

"That brings us to the heart of the matter," said Angela, serious for a moment.

"It does?" said Matthew, swallowing hard.

"Yes, my home is where the problem lies and why you two were sent here."

# Chapter 7

"Follow me," said Angela. "I'll show you where I live." After swimming for a while, a large, dark creature appeared in the distance. It seemed to have long tentacles that were reaching out to grab whatever swam by. The closer they got to it, the more they realized it wasn't living but was man-made. It was a shipwreck.

"Wow!" said Matthew already thinking about sunken treasure. Anna was thinking about the ship too, only she was imagining dangerous creatures lurking inside among the skeletons of dead bodies that they would surely find. It gave her the shivers, and she stayed right behind her brother for protection.

Sensing Anna's fear, Angela said, "Don't worry about anything in the daytime. It's at night when we really need your help."

"What happens at night?" asked Matthew.

"That's when the ghost appears and scares us all. It's impossible to sleep when she starts haunting us."

"A ghost!" cried Anna. She couldn't decide if a ghost would be better than the creatures she was imagining. "How can we help with a ghost?"

"You two have been hand-picked because of certain qualities and talents you have. Anna, you are able to draw nearly anything—right?"

"I guess so," admitted Anna.

"And Matthew, your intelligence is essential here. We will work together with many others you haven't met yet. We will work as a team to solve the mystery and send the ghost on her way so our home can be peaceful."

"I don't get it," said Matthew.

"You will. Just be patient. Now, how about some Krabby patties?"

The clear blue Caribbean Sea had changed color. Dusk was upon them, making it more difficult to see. As they made their way from Bikini Bottom, the activity level in the world around them was changing. Angela said it was because some types of fish slept during the night, while others did their feeding then. Angela brought the brother and sister back to the shipwreck and to the guest room she had prepared. It was very dark now, and Matthew and Anna were ready to sleep. Tomorrow they would get to explore the entire wreck and hopefully learn why the sea creatures needed their help. The warm sea current lulled them to sleep.

The sun's rays made their way through fathoms of water to the ocean floor. The bright light and clear water made it possible for the humans to get a good look at the wreck of the Rosa Marie. It lay sadly on the ocean floor with a large hole punched into its bow. The masts had been broken and lay extending sideways from the deck—the tentacles Anna had imagined. The enormous cotton sails had long ago rotted and hung in narrow shreds like badly dressed Halloween ghosts.

"Does anyone down here know anything about the ship?" asked Matthew.

"The schoolmaster fish knows a few things about it."

"Where can I find him?"

"In his classroom. Where else? Judging by the sun, he will be teaching soon. Yes, yes, I'm right, see that grouper fish over there?" Anna and Matthew turned to see a large fish with dozens of smaller ones.

"The grouper is grouping the fish into their appropriate schools so they can head over to their classrooms, to the schoolmaster."

"Fascinating!" said Matthew.

All at once, a trumpet fish sounded an alarm. Instantly, there was a frenzy as the once calm ocean became a scurry of activity. Fish darted into the coral, between rocks, and into the shipwreck for protection.

"What did the trumpet fish say?" asked Anna, who was scared and next to tears.

"Don't worry, Anna. A shark was spotted. But the sergeant major fish and his soldier fish were alerted, and they will start patrolling to find out where the shark is and keep it out of our neighborhood if it gets too close. I told you; we look out for each other."

"Let's talk more about the ship," said Matthew, still thinking about the buried treasure.

"Good idea. How about I quickly go and ask the schoolmaster what he knows? It will disrupt classes less if I go alone. In the meantime, feel free to explore the wreck."

"Explore the wreck? Do you think it's safe?" asked Anna.

"I think so because Angela wouldn't take us here if it wasn't," reasoned Matthew.

"Okay, but let's stay close together."

The wreck rooted in the sea bottom was enormous, but it didn't look much like a ship anymore. It was listing to the port side, and during the more than two hundred years it had been there, every inch of it was crusted with barnacles and other animal and plant life.

"It has been made into its own ecosystem," said Matthew.

"An eco-what?" asked Anna.

"Because so many plants and animals call it home, it has become its own little community—an ecosystem." The pair first swam all around the exterior of the ship to get their bearings. "I'm trying to figure out how this ship would look if it were in good shape," said Matthew. "Now that we know the ship's name, I'm going to use Google and see if there is any information about it."

"How will your phone work down here?" asked

Anna, sensibly. "Phones don't work underwater."

"That's true. But so far, lots of things have been doing what we wouldn't think they could, so I'm going to try it." Matthew dug his phone out of his wetsuit and turned it on. To the children's surprise, it fired up and connected to the Internet. Unfortunately, there wasn't a great deal of information about the ship's journey or its sinking. But when Matthew read it was transporting silver and gems back from New Spain to Europe, he got very excited. There might be buried treasure after all! The web said the cause of the sinking was never established, but the best educated guess was that it had been attacked by pirates hoping to find riches aboard. Matthew's heart sunk; perhaps the pirates had stolen everything of value.

The pair continued swimming and investigating various areas of the ship. They knew they must be in what was the galley. There were remnants of cooking and eating utensils half buried in the sand, rusted and corroded but still recognizable. Several of the small cabins were in one piece although many aquatic plants and animals were now calling them home.

Other than some dish shards, the children couldn't find anything of value or any clue as to why they had been brought to help. Angela returned from her conversation with the schoolmaster fish. Although he didn't possess the kind of information Matthew had found on the Internet, he had stories about the wreck that had been handed down from one fish generation to the next. This knowledge could prove priceless, and Matthew was eager to hear the details.

"The schoolmaster fish said the story told to him by his great-great-grandfather was that there had been a tremendous storm, likely a hurricane, which caused the Rosa Marie to sink. He said there never were any pirate ship sightings in the area by the flying fish or the sea turtles during that time. And as far as he knows, very few divers have bothered with the wreckage." This new data thrilled Matthew. Now he had something to go on, a place to start his investigation. But how could he help the sea creatures when he didn't know what the crux of the problem was?

"Angela, you said something about a ghost. How can we help?"

"I haven't said much about it for two reasons. One is because I didn't want to scare you two off, and the second reason is because we aren't sure why we have the problem."

"First thing's first," said Matthew rationally. "What is it that may scare us off—the ghost?"

Angela took a big breath and let out dozens of bubbles before she began to explain. "Yes, it has been around for hundreds of years. It never says much, just appears whenever it wants. That's the worst of it. At night, we never know whether it's going to bother us or not. None of us get much sleep. We are always watching for it."

"Are you sure it's a real ghost, not just a jellyfish or another sea creature?"

"Oh, it's a ghost all right. We see her all the time."

"Where?" asked Matthew

"Always in the shipwreck—but not always in the same place. I've seen her plenty of times, and she seems upset about something, sad and anxious, sort of."

"Do you think she's trying to scare you or hurt you?" asked Anna.

"No, she seems like she needs help or is trying to tell us something. I'm not as afraid as some of the fish. Many are terrified. She has caused a lot of panic, and many sea creatures have left our neighborhood because of her. I first heard about her from my grandfather, and everything he told me I have seen for myself."

"Hmm," said Matthew, taking it all in while Anna stood by mesmerized with eyes as big as saucers. "How does everyone describe her?"

"She is a lady in her forties and is dressed in a long green fancy dress. Her hair is dark and is pulled back on top of her head. She wears a fancy green hat to match her dress."

"Sounds as though she's dressed like they did in the 1800s, and that's when the ship sunk."

"We think she died on the ship, but we don't know why she is still here."

"This sounds like a cool mystery to solve," said Matthew excitedly while Anna could only think of the possibility of a real dead ghost.

"I'm going to do more research about the Rosa Marie to begin with," explained Matthew. "I guess we should stick close to the ship in case she appears."

"Well, you could stick nearby, but I'm certain she will contact you when she needs to, no matter where you are," said Angela.

"Anybody hungry?" asked Matthew.

"Yes!" said Anna.

"Let's head to Bikini Bottom."

While waiting for their meals, Angela asked other restaurant patrons to tell their stories about the ghost to their visitors. To pass the time while waiting for their food, Anna began to draw on her placemat. She sketched the salt shaker that sat on the table, and miraculously the shaker became real. Not believing her eyes, she drew a fork, and it appeared to come off the paper and into reality. Anna poked Matthew and showed him her newfound power. The children and Angela agreed Anna had been given the power for the purpose of helping to figure out the ghost mystery.

On the way back to the wreck, Angela was able to introduce the children to more of her friends and neighbors.

"Hi, family," said Angela looking down to the sea bottom.

"Who did you say 'hi' to?" asked Anna. "I didn't see anything."

"Oh, I said 'hi' to Mr. and Mrs. Sand Dollar and Sand Nickel. Families used to have sand pennies too, but they were phased out—they became quite insignificant. Here comes my friend, Printer. He is a squid."

"Hi, Angela, how are you?" asked Printer.

"Hi, Printer, I'm doing well. What are you up to?" asked Angela.

"I'm on my way to a document signing. See you later."

"Have a good day!" said Angela as the squid thrust himself farther away. "He can squirt black ink, so he is valuable when it comes to having documents signed," explained the angel fish. Matthew just shook his head. The things he was learning were amazing.

Much of the area around the shipwreck was becoming familiar to the children. Anna and Matthew both thought they could find their way around the neighborhood on their own. Even some of the sea creatures could now call the children by name as they passed by. Angela left the siblings to explore on their own. They headed to the amazing coral reef with its astounding beauty. Many small animals lived among the coral. Matthew, having studied the sea in school, could identify sea sponges and anemone. They were continuing to enjoy exploring when a trumpet fish made an announcement, "Ghost sighting! Attention, ghost sighting!" Matthew didn't know if the announcement had been made for their benefit, but he wasn't about to waste the opportunity. He grabbed Anna's hand and, with her mermaid tail, she was able to swim at top speed back to the wreck.

# Chapter 8

The warning provoked two reactions. Some of the creatures swam as fast as they could for cover while others did what Anna and Matthew did—headed for the wreck and hopefully, the ghost. By the time they arrived at the ship, there was no sign of her. The children and Angela were disappointed. If the mystery was ever to be solved, the ghost was going to have to appear and communicate. They had no choice but be patient until dark. Perhaps the ghost would come back. Out of the corner of her eye, Anna saw something she had never seen before. She scooted out of the wreck to get a better look.

"I see you've spotted my friends, Bridle and Spur; and yes, they are seahorses. I believe they are on their way to a rodeo," informed Angela.

"Fish don't have rodeos!" exclaimed Anna.

"Of course, we do. Not everyone participates including me. It's not my thing. I like to go and watch. Would you and Matthew care to see what it's all about?"

"I would," said Anna.

"Don't go without me!" added Matthew. A short swim later, they arrived at the rodeo. When

Matthew saw there were no bleachers, he wondered where they would sit.

"If you're a fish, you don't worry about sitting down," reminded Angela.

"And if you are with me, you don't have to worry about it either," retorted Anna as she drew a couple of seats in the sand. One was a chair for Matthew, and her mermaid tail fit just right on the chaise, complete with cup holder—which made them all laugh. It seemed the rodeo was well underway by the time the trio had arrived, but judging by the program, there was still plenty more to see. The first competition they saw was with the groupers. They had to herd catfish into a corral, and the grouper with the shortest time won the event and moved on to the semi-final. Matthew howled with laughter at this event, but he had to explain to Anna why it was so funny.

"We humans have a saying, when something is difficult, it's like herding cats. Here they use catfish; just too hilarious," laughed Matthew as he slapped his knee for effect. The groupers completed their herding, and next, the spectators saw scallops entering the arena.

"Scallops? What can they do?" asked Anna.

"They don't move around much—they stack on top of each other so the seahorses can race around them."

"You mean like barrel racing?"

"I guess so," said Angela not really knowing what barrels were. As the kids watched the racing, they informed Angela that it was exactly like barrel racing. The little sea horses were very quick, but unfortunately, they couldn't pick out Bridle or Spur from the rest. They all seemed to look the same. The next event featured cowfish and buffalo fish riding. The first heat had contestants riding cowfish. Then subsequent heats saw them riding more energetic and aggressive buffalo fish. Luckily, when the contestants were bucked off and put in danger, the clown fish came out to divert attention away so the rider could make his escape. The last event was open to all octopi. The contestants had a series of challenges to perform showing their agility at using all eight of their arms at the same time. They had to use a keyboard and type something that made sense, stack plastic cups, and throw marbles into cups, just to name a few tasks. The winner was amazing, somehow managing to keep control of all eight arms at once.

Before going back to the wreck, they stopped to eat at the Krusty Krab food truck that was parked at the rodeo. There they saw Squidward with a medal around his neck. They missed seeing him compete but learned he had won the ink squirting contest against eight other squids. What a fun day it had been. Now it was time for some relaxation and ghost watching at the wreck.

The sun was setting and the undersea neighborhood was getting dark. The sea creatures all headed to bed except, of course, the Night Sargent, sergeant major, and soldier fish, who were beginning their patrols to keep watch for nighttime predators. Anna had drawn waterbeds for herself and Matthew, and they were just drifting off to sleep when all the light from above disappeared. Anna thought of her parents, missing them a little, but then remembered that Angela had assured them time was standing still on board the Disney ship so the children would not be missed by their parents. Anna could feel the gentle swaying of the current when the rhythm was interrupted, causing her to stir. She turned over and opened her eyes briefly to see the ghost sitting at the end of her bed. Anna opened her mouth to scream, but all that came out were bubbles.

The lady ghost really didn't look that scary; in fact, she reminded Anna of pictures of her great, great grandmother. The ghost extended her hand toward Anna, and Anna extended hers toward the lady as a sign of friendship. It seemed the lady in green could not speak, but she kept pointing to Anna's head. Anna needed help so she called for Matthew. Even together, they were confused by the ghost's carrying on, and eventually, maybe out of frustration, the ghost faded away.

"What do you think she wanted?" asked Anna.

"I'm not sure but I need to do more research about her and this ship," concluded Matthew. Come morning, the children shared their nighttime experience with Angela.

"I think I might have been scared if I were you," admitted Angela.

"But you're an angel. Don't you have protective powers?"

"I have some. But usually when the ghost appears, we call my mom."

"Why is that?"

"I'm an angel fish, but my mom is a queen angel fish, so she has super powers compared to me."

"We didn't feel like we needed protection—the ghost wasn't very scary, and it seemed she was trying to tell us something. We have no idea what, so Matthew is going to do a little more research to see if we can figure it out." Meanwhile, Matthew had connected to the Internet and through some intensive searching, had come up with some new information about the Rosa Marie and her voyage. It took several days and multiple websites to get enough information to be able to understand the nature of its journey. Because the ship had been used to acquire a new crown for a European queen, more was known and written about it than most parcel ship crossings of the Atlantic.

The lady ghost did not make another appearance for several days. By then, they had accumulated more knowledge about the ship, but even the new information didn't explain why the ghost kept appearing and causing alarm to the skittish fish. Matthew and Anna sat down one day and began to discuss the wreck. It seemed one of the misconceptions was that pirates had sunk the ship and stolen the treasure. But that was in contrast to what the schoolmaster fish had insisted. So now, Matthew was going to try and find out, once and for all, how the shipwreck happened. He figured he had to search weather for that part of the Caribbean during that time period. The hull of the wreckage had a large hole in it that could have been caused by a cannon ball, but Matthew reasoned while the ship was sinking due to a storm, the hole might have been caused by hitting rocks. So, the question remained, what came first, the hole or the sinking?

# Chapter 9

It was as though the lady dressed in green knew that the children had some unanswered questions. She reappeared to Matthew, this time, several hours after he was in bed, and although he was somewhat nervous around her, he needed to get some much-needed answers. From his research on www.fishstories.com, it seemed that the stories the schoolmaster fish had heard were true. Pirates had not been involved. Just to confirm what he had read, he asked the ghost if pirates had sunk the ship and stolen the booty. The ghost's response was puzzling; she slowly faded away. Matthew was disappointed. He needed information, and he needed it from the ghost. The next time the ghost appeared to him, he asked two very simple questions that he already knew the answer to.

"Are you dead?" asked Matthew. The lady answered by becoming brighter and in sharper focus.

"Do you need us to help you?" The lady remained bright.

"Were any members of your family on the ship with you?" This time the lady began to fade. Now,

Matthew thought he had figured out a way to communicate with the ghost. This would make everything easier. Full of excitement, he called Anna and Angela.

"Anna and Angela, the lady is here." Both swam quickly to his side. He explained to them that he had discovered how to communicate with the ghost. As Matthew turned back to the ghost, she was gone. It seemed the ghost was fussy about when and who she dealt with. Finding out important details about the mystery would be easy if they could ask the ghost questions and understand the answers. They needed to think ahead and make a list of the things they needed to ask.

"Wish we had paper and pencil," said Matthew.

"Your wish is my command," smiled Anna. She bent down and drew two pieces of paper and two sharpened pencils. Voila! Instantly the drawings turned to real objects. The kids sat on their chairs and began to write down all the useful questions they could ask.

Before long, it was dusk. Then night settled upon the ocean. The children lay down to sleep, but neither could close their eyes for fear of missing a ghost visit. They were not disappointed. Several hours after going to bed, she appeared once again to Matthew. This time, he didn't feel nervous, only anxious to get the answers to the questions he and Anna had written down. Matthew wanted the ghost to know that he and Anna were eager to help, so he explained that he was going to ask many questions. He didn't dare take time out to awaken Anna for fear the ghost would leave, so he fired off question after question, and the ghost responded to each one.

From the strange conversation, they had, Matthew learned the ship had not been attacked by pirates but by a hurricane. He also learned there had been no survivors, and that many riches had been on board. The ghost confirmed that it was the queen's new crown that the ghost wanted them to find and take to Europe. She also admitted that the missing crown was the reason for her ghostly appearances over the past two hundred years. She faded away after the last answer, and Matthew whooped for joy. Now he knew what they were looking for! Anna and Angela hadn't stirred, and Matthew lay back down to think about what he had just learned. Finding the crown would not be easy, especially after two hundred years. The ocean bottom, shifting currents, and sea life were only some of the challenges they would face.

The brilliant morning sun shone through the water and lit up the undersea world. Many of the creatures began to wake up and look for breakfast, including Angela and Anna. Once Matthew saw the pair was awake, he wasted no time in sharing the information the lady ghost had given him. It would be important to come up with a plan so they could systematically search the ocean floor as well as everything within the sunken ship. Matthew Googled how to explore a dive site and came up with a plan. They would need to recruit some help, and Angela assured them there would be plenty of friends and neighbors willing to assist if it meant getting rid of the ghost forever and putting her soul to rest so she finally had peace.

Matthew knew that finding the crown would be very difficult it if wasn't inside the vessel. They would start there, beginning at the top and working their way down to the hull. Now they would need to find some extra fish power.

"What kind of additional help are you looking for?" asked Angela.

"It's very dark down there, especially inside the hull. There is a lot of broken wood and other things, so we have to be very careful, and it would be safest to only work during daylight."

"I have some friends that will be very useful," said Angela. "I'm going to swim over to them and see if they are available to help." Angela quickly swam away, not divulging who the friends were or how they could be helpful.

"Anna, how about you and I swim up to the top of the ship and start there? At least there is some light. Now remember, the wood is very rotten so try not to put any weight on it." Anna laughed and wiggled her tail at her brother. "Oh yeah, I guess you can't stand on it even if you tried," remembered Matthew.

"Even though it's daytime, it's still a little hard to see. I wonder if anyone has flashlights. We will have to ask Angela. Everything is sprawled all over the place. It's going to take a lot of time to look in, around, and under everything," said Anna, sizing up the task before them.

"It's going to be worse below deck. It's much darker, and there is so much more debris down there."

"One good thing is that everything seems to weigh less in the water, so moving heavy stuff might not be that hard," said Anna. "But one challenge is that everything is covered in barnacles making it difficult to know what some objects even are."

Angela reappeared with some lamp fish. Anna wasn't very impressed at first—they were not big, and their faces were quite ugly. They had plenty of small spiny teeth, and their scales were red and brown and white. Angela had not brought them for their beauty; she had summoned them because of their useful ability to produce light. The fish were small, perfect for getting into tiny spaces. Once Anna learned of their special gift, she was excited for them to help.

"Matthew and Anna, I'd like you to meet the three foremen of the group. This is Watt, Torch, and Beacon. You tell these guys how many fish you need and where. While you are getting the lamp fish organized, I have another group of fish lined up to help. I'm going to get them now." Angela swam off with a wave of her fin while the kids started dividing the living lanterns into two groups. The teams then moved to the upper deck when Angela reappeared with about a dozen blowfish. Angela saw Matthew and Anna looking at the fish's spines and then casting a suspicious look at each other.

"I know what you are thinking," said Angela. "You are worried about getting poisoned by these guys. I promise you both, there is no danger to either of you. I'd like you to meet Gust and his niece, Gale. They are in charge of their group.

"What do you do that can help us?" asked Anna.

"Watch this," said Gust as he took in a large gulp of water and spewed it out with such force it cleared a small area of the ship's deck right down to the wood. "And we can do the same thing on the ocean floor—hopefully, we will help you uncover what is under the sand and debris," added Gale.

*Yep, these two will come in handy,* said Anna to herself. Matthew and Anna each took a group of the fish helpers and swam back to the top deck of the sunken ship. Just as Anna tried to swim forward to the bow, she was stopped suddenly. Her heart skipped a beat as she realized she was unable to physically move forward. Her first thought was that the green lady ghost was the cause but then she heard a giggle from behind. It was her brother who had stepped on her tail to bring her to a sudden stop.

"Matthew! Stop it!" yelled Anna. "What is the matter with you?"

"Ha-ha. I've wanted to do that to you ever since you grew your tail," laughed Matthew.

"Matthew, you make me so mad," said Anna, finally able to go on her way.

Anna and her crew began at the bow of the boat while Matthew's team started at the stern. The barnacles that clung to all parts of the vessel could not be moved by the blowfish, so Anna drew a couple of scrapers. These proved ideal for getting rid of the crusty critters, allowing them all to continue to search for the ship's booty, especially the crown.

The fish on both teams worked in shifts all day long. They had covered a large part of the upper deck before dark came. Although the lamp fish were sure they could produce enough light to continue digging, the humans needed to call it a day. They were tired and needed to go to bed. Anna had just stretched out on her chaise when an eerie light appeared followed by the lady ghost, who did nothing but smile and then fade away.

# Chapter 10

Scouring the ship was a long and tedious process. With absolutely no clue as to where the loot might have ended up, Matthew and Anna had to take their time and carefully search each part of every deck. Below deck was confining and dark despite the lamp fish. In fact, it took many of the fish to point their lights at the same time in order for the kids to see much of anything. One day was like the next, first assembling all the helper fish. Then carrying on where they had left off the day before. Matthew and Anna thought lovingly of their parents every once in a while. They didn't completely understand what Angela had meant by "time was standing still" on the ship while they carried on with their adventure, but she had assured them there was nothing for them to fear, nor would their parents have a chance to worry about them. This made them feel secure and allowed them to concentrate on and enjoy the mystery at hand.

It seemed that each time they became discouraged, the ghost would appear, nearly scaring the fish to death but encouraging the kids to keep going. The deconstruction site became a topic of conversation and debate. Some fish thought that messing up the wreck was a bad idea. Many creatures had made the sunken ship their home, and now it was being torn apart, displacing those fish and their families. But in the end, they decided that if finding the treasure would stop the ghost from continuing to appear, the peace of mind would be well worth the temporary discombobulation.

One day, while working in the blackness of the ship's hull, Matthew turned around to find himself face to face with a pair of eyes the size of grapefruit. The huge creature had tentacles with flashing lights that were coming closer and closer. He screamed but had nowhere to go as he was completely surrounded by the monsters. He froze in terror, his heart beating out of control, and his legs went weak like rubber. Anna heard his screams and swam over to him. She stayed back a ways, treading water, and laughed until she cried. Many of the helper fish roared with laughter too. Matthew didn't get it. What was so funny? He was surrounded by glowing monsters that appeared threatening.

"Help," said Matthew, weakly.

"What? You don't like being afraid?" teased Anna. "Okay, guys, I think you can back off. I think you scared him enough—good job!"

"You told them to come and scare me? That's mean," said Matthew still shaking.

"About as mean as playing tricks on me," she reminded him.

"What are these?"

"More friends of mine," admitted Angela. "That's Reach and his family. They are glowing squids—huge glowing squids. I think Reach is about six feet long."

"No more tricks, Anna, I promise," said Matthew, shuddering just thinking what would have happened if they had all attacked him.

Finally, one day, they found a single silver and gold coin buried in the hull under much sand and debris. It wasn't much, but it was enough to raise the spirits of the work crew and give them hope that there was more to be found. Matthew's team had uncovered the coin, and it was decided by a fish vote that everything they discovered would be stockpiled until they could decide what to do with the loot.

The silver coin was only the beginning. Other coins were found in many locations, on and off the ship, at many depths under the sand. Both types of worker fish were invaluable during the treasure hunt, and Matthew and Anna soon knew all their names and personalities. By now, dozens of coins had been found as well as a couple of silver bars, but the crown's whereabouts remained a mystery. Matthew had plotted the locations of all the silver they had located so far. It seemed that the coins, at one time, had been together in some sort of container, but as the ship was tossed and sunk, the coins were scattered—he could see some sort of path they had made to the ship. Thinking about what the weight of the crown might be compared to the coins, he concluded it would have sunk first. Because of its weight, it may not have been so affected by the undersea currents. He was quite sure that where the ship sat on the ocean bottom was not where it had started to sink.

From the Internet, he knew the size of the Rosa Marie, its route, how many passengers and crew had been on board, and the type of cargo it was carrying back to Europe. All of this information made it possible for Matthew to think about how long it would have taken it to sink and then settle to where it now lay. He explained all of this as best as he could to those involved in the search, and they decided to explore the ocean bottom away from the wreck—southwest of the ship, to be exact. Matthew stayed up long after everyone had fallen asleep. By the light of his phone, he sketched, did math, and came up with an educated guess as to where they should concentrate their efforts next. Matthew was so excited to begin excavating the new area, he had difficulty sleeping. Just as soon as the Caribbean sun began to slice through the water, he was shaking Anna awake, anxious to show her his hand-drawn map and location calculations.

"Anna, Anna, wake up," pleaded her brother.

"What's wrong?" asked Anna.

"Nothing is wrong. I figured out where we should look next."

"Is that all?" asked Anna flicking her tail hard, causing a strong current that sent Matthew floating away.

Ignoring his sister's obvious annoyance, he insisted, "C'mon and get up, soon the helper fish will be here anyway."

"Jeez, Matthew, you can be such a pain. All right, show me what you have figured out and why." As Matthew began to explain his calculations to Anna, Angel and the helper fish began to arrive. They seemed excited to try a new area, especially after hearing Matthew's reasons for choosing it. The work crew swam together to where Matthew insisted they begin their day. It was far from the wreck. In fact, some of the helper fish had never been this far from home before. They weren't in hostile territory, but they were strangers here. Many curious fish began to emerge, wondering what was going on. Angela asked a passing blue tang to find the leader or spokesperson for the neighborhood so she could explain their presence. At first, wary of the newcomers, they became excited when Anna and Matthew spoke to them. However, by the end of the day, creatures in the new neighborhood were thrilled to think the crown might be in their backyard, and they offered to help.

The work continued, and the crew began to feel very at home in the adjacent area. Creatures from the shipwreck neighborhood would often make the trek to see how the crew was doing. This enabled the inhabitants from both sites to visit and get to know each other. One day, a local restaurant invited the workers to come and eat lunch. Matthew and Anna had decided on a wonderful sounding salad made with many local greens. The menu said it would be made tableside. When the waiter arrived, on his cart sat a very unusual vessel in which he would toss the salad. It didn't appear to be a salad bowl but more of a case. It was made of very sturdy leather and was opened by unbuckling two leather tooled straps. When Anna asked about it, the octopus waiter said the restaurant had had it for hundreds of years, but he didn't know anything else about it. The kids asked to see the owner to find out more information, but the owner said it had been handed down to the restaurant owner's family for a very long time after someone found it on the ocean floor many generations ago.

The new information made Anna and Matthew think. It was certainly made by humans, it could have come off the Rosa Marie, and it could have held a crown! It was yet another clue that fueled the crew to keep searching. Matthew reached for his phone to take a picture of the odd salad server. The next time the ghost appeared, he would be sure to ask if she recognized it.

That opportunity came three nights later. Just as the kids were settling down for the night, the familiar glow in the distance became brighter. Anna was glad to see her this time. Because of the historical research, Matthew had done, they could call her by name.

"Is your name Mary?" asked Anna. The apparition glowed so brightly it was nearly blinding.

Mary's answer made the children jump up and down with joy. They were on the right path. When they showed her the photo of the leather case, they swore they saw tears running down her cheeks.

The crown was eventually found nowhere near the sunken ship. As Matthew, had projected, it had fallen completely off the ship during its sinking. They had dug about a foot into the ocean floor's sand when they came upon a heavy object. Assuming it was just another artifact, no one was excited until it was completely uncovered by Anna. It took a few seconds before she understood what lay before her and several seconds longer before she could find her voice and holler for Matthew.

"Matthew, Matthew, I found it!" Her lamp fish flashed their lights, and the blowfish blew thousands of bubbles in celebration. Matthew swam rapidly to see what Anna had found. He couldn't believe it when he saw what looked like a crown. He lifted it out of Anna's hands, surprised at how heavy it was. After looking it over, everyone was amazed at the condition it was in. Being buried in the sand had kept it free from barnacles, but, of course, it needed a good polish; surprisingly, each and every gem was in place. Mary did not wait until the kids were back on the ship to resurface. She appeared and hovered over them right there and then to the horror of those that had never seen or heard of her before. But this time she seemed different, happy and excited.

# Chapter 11

"Now what?" Anna asked Matthew the next morning. "We found the crown. Now what do we do with it?"

"I don't know. I'm hoping Mary will tell us. It belongs to the royal family that Mary worked for."

"Do you think she wants us to return it to them?" And with that, Mary appeared.

"Mary, we were wondering what you want us to do with the crown. Did you want it taken to Europe?" Mary became very bright—her way of saying yes. Now the siblings had another challenge—how to get the crown across the ocean.

"I don't know how we can do that," said Matthew shaking his head.

"What's going on, guys? Neither of you look happy. You should be excited," said Angela.

"We are excited. Excited that the crown has been found, but the ghost wants the crown taken across the Atlantic to Europe. Back to the family it belongs to. How are we going to do that?"

"Across the ocean, you say," said Angela trying to think of a strategy. "How good are you at drawing boats?" asked Angela.

"Not that good. It would take a really big boat to go that far."

"Could you draw a plane?"

"A plane would be easier," admitted Anna.

"See what you can do. I know some pilots."

"Wow! You have a lot of impressive friends," commented Matthew.

"Have you heard of flying fish?" asked Angela.

"Of course," said Matthew, "but I thought..."

"I know, you thought they fly over the water, and they do, but they also know how to fly planes. That's why they are called flying fish."

"I never knew that," said Anna. It was decided that a plane would be needed and that the brother and sister would accompany the crown back to Europe. The first plane Anna drew was a prop plane.

"I think we need a jet, Anna," said Matthew.

"Show me a picture of one on your phone, and I'll copy it." She drew a private jet that looked just right.

"If the pilots are willing, we could leave tomorrow." With the important decisions made, all that had been involved with solving the mystery of the missing crown made their way to the Krusty Krab for a meal of farewell and celebration. The large group had so much fun bringing up memories that they had made during their time together. The humans and the sea creatures had learned a lot about each other, but now it was time for Matthew and Anna to spend their last night below the sea.

Daylight broke and Matthew and Anna were up early. Today was a big day. They had a long flight ahead of them, and they weren't sure how they would feel being out of the water. Anna had no idea what would happen to her mermaid tail. A large crowd gathered at the spot where the siblings would surface then swim to the shore. All the sea creatures that had assisted in the discovery of the treasure were there to say good-bye. Judging by the crowd, most of the inhabitants of the two neighborhoods also showed up. The kids were overwhelmed by the good wishes. Then Angela swam forward, with Reach beside her.

"Anna and Matthew, there are so many things we want to say to you," said Angela. It has been an amazing experience having you in our world. Because of you, we can go to sleep and not worry about being scared or awakened by the ghost. Not only did you solve a very old mystery but you became our friends."

"It's kind of hard to say good-bye," admitted Anna.

"I agree," Matthew added.

"Before you leave us, we have something for each of you," said Angela, as Reach stepped toward the siblings. "For you, Matthew, we want to give you the very first coin that was ever found. You definitely deserve this." Matthew took it from Reach's tentacle with gratitude. "And for you, wonderful Anna, we have something very special.

"Reach, could you pick up Shuck?" Reach bent

down and gently picked up an oyster that sat on a nearby rock. "Shuck, do you have something to say to Anna?" asked Angela.

"Hi, Anna," said a very tiny voice. "I started making this for you some time ago, and now it's finished." Slowly, Shuck opened her shell, and inside sat a large, shiny pearl. "I hope you like it."

"I love it," said Anna beaming and then blowing a kiss in the direction of the oyster.

"Well, it's time to go," said Matthew. Shouts of good-bye and cheers followed the pair as they swam to the surface. Anna had done a remarkable job of drawing the jet, and they could see it waiting on shore. Just as Anna began splashing her tail, it began to disappear and her feet could be seen. When she stood up and started walking out of the water, each part that was no longer submerged lost its scales and turned back to flesh. By the time they stepped into the jet, all of her scales had disappeared, and Matthew's wet suit was gone too.

"Wow, dude! You flew down that slide-faster than ever before," said Matthew's dad, clapping as Matthew hit the water and slid beneath it. For a moment, Matthew was confused. What had just happened? Could everything that happened beneath the sea have been a dream? It had all happened in the time it took to slide down the waterslide. It had to be Disney magic.

"Oh, Anna, I love the beautiful coral you drew—it looks just like what we saw yesterday," said Anna's mom. Anna looked around, confused. She was sitting on the Disney ship, in the restaurant, having dinner, and her drawing was now being shown on all the monitors. How had she dreamt about the ship wreck and the crown when she hadn't been sleeping? Then she felt her pearl in her pocket and smiled, it hadn't been a dream.

Today was Saturday, and the family had been home from their trip for a week. They missed the ocean and the ship, but later Matthew was going to hockey practice, and Anna was going to a sleepover. First, they had chores to do, and one was to help their dad clean out their fish aquarium. As Dad began to remove the castle and the plants, he wondered outloud, "How did this old coin and this pearl get into the fish tank?" Matthew and Anna kept silently scooping up the colored gravel. When no one owned up to it, their dad said, "Hmm, it must have been a ghost." Anna and Matthew just looked at each other and giggled.

## Author

Rosanna Gartley is the mother of four adult children, four bonus adult children and grandmother to 13. A retired nurse practitioner, she currently lives in southwestern Pennsylvania but hails from the Canadian prairies. Rosanna enjoys her family, most things creative and travelling with her husband, John.

**Title:** *Beads of Courage*®

(Oliver's Story)
- Author: Rosanna Gartley
- Publisher: MouseGate.com
- Paper Back: ISBN: 9781590952269
- eBook: ISBN: 9781590952320
- Number of pages in the finished book: 60
- Publication Date: April 25, 2017

Baby Oliver's life started out precariously in the neonatal intensive care unit. Each day, while he was a patient, his parents were given beads of various shapes and colors. Each bead symbolized a medical procedure that Oliver had endured on that day. By the time Oliver was discharged, his collection of beads was impressive.

As Oliver grew, his Beads of Courage® continued to hang on his bedroom wall. Not only were they a reminder of what he had lived through but also served as an inspiration for future challenges.

You won't want to miss what happens during a family vacation when this amazing little boy employs Disney magic to help those who need a little courage.

**Title:** *Castaway Crown*

(Matthew and Anna's Undersea Adventure)
- Author: Rosanna Gartley
- Publisher: MouseGate.com
- Paper Back: ISBN: 9781590953532
- eBook: ISBN: 9781590953358
- Number of pages in the finished book: 76
- Publication Date: 2018

Matthew and Anna are full of excitement when they learn their family is going on a Disney cruise. With the magic of Disney both children are propelled into an adventure far below the ocean when they are asked to help the sea creatures get rid of a bothersome ghost. With Matthew's above average intellect coupled with Anna's amazing drawing abilities they solve the two-hundred-year old mystery bringing peace to the sea and the ghost.